I0692555

James P. Baxter, Rhode Island Historical Society

Early Voyages to America

A paper read before the Rhode Island Historical Society

James P. Baxter, Rhode Island Historical Society

Early Voyages to America
A paper read before the Rhode Island Historical Society

ISBN/EAN: 9783337381257

Printed in Europe, USA, Canada, Australia, Japan

Cover: Foto ©Andreas Hilbeck / pixelio.de

More available books at **www.hansebooks.com**

Early Voyages to America.

A PAPER READ BEFORE THE

Rhode Island Historical Society

BY

JAMES PHINNEY BAXTER, A. M.

PROVIDENCE :

PRINTED FOR THE SOCIETY

1889.

Note from the Society.

—

This valuable monograph on American history was read by Mr. Baxter, at a meeting of the Rhode Island Historical Society, held in its Cabinet, March 6, 1888, when its author, a corresponding member of the Society, received, on motion of the Hon. Royal C. Taft seconded by the Rev. S. L. Caldwell, D. D., a unanimous vote of thanks for his elaborate and scholarly paper. The branch of the subject relating to the voyages of the Northmen awakened much interest among members of the Society half a century ago, and the general interest therein is illustrated by works published by the Royal Society of Northern Antiquaries at Copenhagen, which, though on the shelves of our library, are practically beyond the reach of most of our members, being in a foreign language with which they are not familiar.

INTRODUCTION.

The following account of Early Voyages to America was prepared in order to place before an audience in a somewhat popular form, a subject requiring for its proper exposition, much larger space and more critical treatment.

This statement should disarm the criticism of scholars, and explain to those who have made an exhaustive study of the various phases of the subject, and to whom nothing that I am able to present can be novel, the *raison d'etre* of this publication, made by friends, who have thought it of sufficient interest to be put in type.

Novelty in the method of identifying places described in the Sagas is disclaimed, and the casual reader is reminded that this branch of the subject is purely conjectural; at the same time, the accuracy with which the Sagas describe localities about and in the vicinity of Rhode Island, Nantucket, Cape Cod and Massachusetts Bay, is so remarkable as to be entitled to most careful consideration.

JAMES PHINNEY BAXTER.

Portland, August, 1889.

EARLY VOYAGES TO AMERICA.

READ BEFORE THE

RHODE ISLAND HISTORICAL SOCIETY,

BY

JAMES PHINNEY BAXTER.

The history of this Continent prior to its discovery by Europeans is veiled in mystery. There are many dim allusions of voyages made to it by adventurers, to be found in ancient writings, but nothing of a strictly definite nature prior to the fifteenth century; for hitherto, the great ocean which beat upon the western shores of Europe, bore appropriately the title of the Sea of Darkness, on account of the absence of knowledge respecting it by the civilized World.

Speculations too chimerical to be profitably considered, have been indulged in by fanciful writers respecting the colonization of our Continent. Athanasias Kircher has given the Egyptians the credit of colonizing it,[1] basing his argument upon the religious worship found here; while Edward Brerewood contends upon linguistic grounds, that the Tartars are entitled to that credit;[2] and Marc Lescarbot, with a faith almost enviable, strives to show, that the Canaanites, driven out by Joshua, emigrated hither ; that Noah was a native of this country, and was borne back to his ancestral home by the flood.[3]

The first really serious attempt, however, to trace geographically a voyage to this Continent, has been made by De Guignes,[4] who, basing his arguments upon the historian Li Yen, contends that the Chinese reached our western shores from Asia in the seventh century. This view has been considered of sufficient importance to engage the attention of several able writers, who have opposed it with varying degrees of ability.[5] That this Continent was inhabited in prehistoric times by a race of men of a very different type from the red men whom our forefathers found here is evident from the remarkable remains which are found so abundantly throughout the West.

Of these earth works particularly, many are of such remarkable extent as to strike the beholder with wonder. Those at Marietta, in Ohio, cover an area of three - fourths of a mile in length by half a mile in breadth, and consist of two immense squares, one containing fifty, and the other twenty-seven acres, the walls of the larger being nearly six feet in height and more than twenty feet broad at the base. Near by is an elliptical structure thirty-five feet high enclosed by a circular wall. Within the larger enclosure are four truncated pyramids ; three being approached by graded passage ways to their summits, and from the south wall runs a graded way to the Muskingum valley six hundred feet in length by over one hundred and fifty feet in breadth. So thick were similar works where the City of St. Louis now stands that it was called Mound City. A group between Alton and St. Louis contained as many as sixty structures."

One of these works in the form of a parallelogram, ninety feet in height, with sides at the base respectively seven hundred and five hundred feet in length, and a terrace on the Southwest one hundred and sixty by three hundred feet, was reached by a graded way, the summit being truncated and affording a platform two hundred by four hundred and fifty feet. Upon this platform was a small mound about ten feet high, containing human bones, vases, and stone implements.

It is supposed that a temple once stood on the platform, and that the rites of the priests could be beheld by the multitudes below. In many of the mounds have been found cists covered with slabs of limestone, enclosing skeletons, and often at the head of the skeletons beautiful specimens of pottery, statuettes, urns and drinking vessels.

Isle Royal and the Northern shores of Lake Superior are the Northwestern limits where these works of a lost people are found. A recent writer says, [7]that "the Mound builders were in the distinctive character of their structures, as marked a people as the Pelasgi, whose prehistoric works can yet be traced throughout Greece and Italy. These Pelasgi were the Wall Builders, for wherever they went they threw up fortifications made of polygonal blocks. So we can trace the Mound builders by their structures from the shores of the great lakes to the milder regions of the Gulf of Mexico and Central America."

Besides articles of pottery often of elegant designs, there are found in the mounds remains of textile fabrics. The Indians found here by the early voyagers did not possess such articles, nor were they capable of erecting such works ; but if any farther proofs were wanting that they were not the builders of these mounds, it would be found in the character of the skulls found in them, which craniologists declare are entirely unlike those of the red men ; but whence these people came, or to what race they belonged, is at present unknown.

To attempt to unravel these mysteries is not our present purpose, nor to indulge in speculations regarding them, which have already been too abundant. We have called attention briefly to the claims of Kircher, Brerewood, Lescarbot, and De Guignes, respecting the first voyagers hither from the eastern hemisphere, and we now come to another claim in favor of a Scandinavian occupation of our eastern shores as early as the latter part of the tenth century.

The first allusion to this subject was made in the ecclesiastical history of Adam von Bremen, written previous to the year 1073.[8] Early in the thirteenth century the Chronicles of the Kings of Norway were written,[9] when it was again alluded to. It was not, however, until 1705, that Thormodus Torfeus treated the subject particularly :[10] yet it failed to attract attention until about fifty years ago, when historical students began to study it.

About this time the Royal Society of Northern Antiquaries began its investigations of old manuscripts which
might throw light upon history and antiquities. Among
these manuscripts were certain Sagas containing accounts
of voyages made to a western land, called Vinland.

The Saga grew out of a desire to perpetuate the memory
of great achievements, and was at first oral. That they
might run smoothly and be more readily committed to memory, many were turned into poetic measure by Saga-men.

These Saga-men were *the literati* of their time, and
were trained to relate accurately and in an attractive manner,
the traditional history of the past. The events related in
the Sagas with which we have to do, took place mostly during the early part of the eleventh century ; but written language had not been introduced into Iceland until about the
middle of the twelfth century, or about a century and a half
after these events took place. It was so difficult, however,
to obtain prepared skins, and the process of writing was so
slow and costly, that not many Sagas were written out until
the thirteenth century. These written Sagas were subse-
quently collected and placed in the libraries of Copenhagen
and Stockholm.

A great variety of subjects are treated in these Sagas,
which comprise poems, stories, memoirs and historical narratives ; but it is as easy to distinguish history from fiction in
these ancient works as it is in modern ones.

Of course, in the Sagas occasionally occur statements of
a somewhat marvelous nature, but not more so than in the

accounts of voyages of a much later date, which are regarded as history; indeed, for the most part, the narratives are given in such a simple and natural manner, and with such an apparent regard for strict accuracy, as to commend themselves to the reader. The most minute incidents are carefully related, and events based upon mere hearsay are given as such."

At first the claims of the Swedish Antiquaries met with vigorous opposition. Their opponents contended in some cases, that there should have been found well defined remains of a Scandinavian occupation if there had been one, and even appealed to the works of the mound builders as examples to show that the inhabitants of a country, if they become extinct, leave behind them works to bear witness to their former existence.

This argument, however, lacked force, since the Scandinavians were not in the habit of building earth works, —the most permanent under certain conditions of the works of man,—and as it is not claimed that they ever made any considerable settlements here, it is hardly to be supposed, that such structures as they would have been likely to erect, would survive the destroying energy of three centuries, amid a barbarous and destructive people.

We know that the settlement at the mouth of the Sagadahoc by the Popham Colonists, which consisted of a fort and fifty habitations, wholly disappeared within a century; as well as Christopher Levet's strong house in Portland Harbor, and other similar structures in New England.

But the enthusiastic advocates of a Scandinavian occupancy of the American Continent were looking about them for such evidences as their opponents required to satisfy their doubt, and the first object which engaged their attention was the old tower at Newport,

"My Stone built Windmill"—in will of Gov. Arnold, Newport, R. I.

which so well represents the mode of building by the Norse people of about the twelfth century, and concerning the origin of which no satisfactory explanation existed until recently ;

but we now know that it was built by Governor Benedict
Arnold, about the year 1676,[12] and was copied from a
similar structure still standing in his native town in England.

Mill at the early home of Gov. Benedict Arnold, Chesterton, England.

This was followed by the discovery, near Fall River,
of the skeleton of a man, who had apparently been
buried in armor. A part of the breast-plate found with
this skeleton was at once forwarded for analysis to
Berzelius, the noted Swedish chemist. Berzelius pro-

nounced it to be similar to Northern armor of the tenth century, and his analysis showed it to be composed of zinc, copper, lead, tin and iron, a composition nearly identical with that of the bronze of that period.

Attention was also directed to the body which the Pilgrims dug up shortly after their landing, which is spoken of by Bradford, and is also to be found in Mourts' Relation.[13]

"The next morning we followed certain beaten pathes and tracts of the Indians into the woods,—as we came into the plaine ground we found a place like a grave, but it was much bigger and longer than any we had yet seen. It was also covered with boards, so as we mused what it should be, and resolved to digge it up, where we found, first a Matt and under that a faire Bow, and then another Matt, and under that a boord about three quarters long, finely carved and paynted, with three tynes or brooches on the top like a Crowne ; also, between the Matts we found Boules, Trayes, Dishes and such like Trinkets ; at length we came to a faire new Matt, and under that two bundles, the one bigger, the other lesse. We opened the greater and found in it a great quantity of fine and perfect red Powder, and in it the bones and skull of a man. The skull had fine yellow haire still on it, and some of the flesh was consumed ; there was bound up with it a knife, a pack needle and two or three old iron things.

It was bound up in a saylers canvas casake, and a payre of cloth breeches ; the red powder was a kind of Embaulment, and yeelded a strong but no offensive smell : It was as fine as any flower. We opened the lesse bundle likewise, and found of the same powder in it, and the bones and head of a little childe, about the leggs and other parts of it was bound strings, and bracelets of fine white Beads ; there was also by it, a little bow, about three quarters long, and some other odd knackes ; we brought sundry of the prettiest things away with us, and covered the corps up againe.

There was varietie of opinions amongst us about the embalmed person ; some thought it was an Indian Lord or King ; others sayd, the Indians have all blacke hayre, and never any was seene with browne or yellow hayre ; some thought it was a Christian of some special note, which had dyed amongst them, and they thus buried him to honor him."

Those who claimed that this was the body of a Norseman called attention to the yellow hair, which so much excited the wonder of the Pilgrims, and which is the distinguishing mark of the Scandinavian people, and insisted that the piece of wood "three quarters long, finely carved and paynted, with three tynes or brooches on the top like a crowne," was the three tined staff called the rymstock or runic staff of the Norsemen.

The mode of burial, too, with mats and domestic utensils, they claimed to be identical with the mode of burial among these people. When asked to account for the new mat they replied, "The body was embalmed and still nothing hardly but the skeleton was remaining, and therefore the statement must be wrong in this respect.

Doubtless this skeleton was in soil near some lime stone spring, or of a nature to preserve it for a long time, as well as the textile fabrics, it being well known that such things have been preserved for ages in favorable localities." Hence,

they said, "some of the things may have appeared newer by
comparison, while the very circumstances of the case show
that they could not have been new."

Copyright, 1882, by Harper & Brothers.

From Harper's Magazine.

But the Dighton Rock of all these supposed relics of
Norse origin, furnished in the estimation of the advocates of
a Scandinavian occupation the best evidence in support of
their claims.[14]

Runic scholars pronounced it a genuine relic, and Prof. Rafn, in the first glow of zeal, gave the World a translation. This rock is on the shore of Taunton River, and has been a puzzle to antiquarians.

Prof. Rafn has translated it as follows : " Thorfinn, with one hundred and fifty-one Norse sea-faring men, took possession of this land."

Edward Everett, in the North American Review, said after studying the subject, " That the rock contains some rude delineations of the figures of men and animals is apparent on the first inspection. The import of the other delineations and characters is more open to doubt. By some persons the characters are regarded as Phœnician. The late Mr. Samuel Harris, a very learned Orientalist, thought he found the Hebrew word *melek* (King) in these characters.

Colonel Vallancy considers them to be Scythian, and Messrs. Rafn and Magnussen think them undoubtedly Runic. In this great diversity of judgment, a decision is extremely difficult."[15] Everett's opinion is probably that of most students to-day.

A curious allusion to the Dighton Rock is to be found in the Sloane Manuscripts in the British Museum, and should be noted. In a letter to Sir Hans Sloane, from Cambridge, December 18, 1730, are drawings of the inscriptions upon the rock made by the Rev. Mr. Fisher and others, and this statement : " There was a Tradition current among ye Eldest Indians that there came a Wooden House (and men of another country in it) who fought ye Indians with mighty success, &c." " This," says the writer, " I think evidently shows that this monument was esteemed by ye Oldest Indians, not only very antique, but a Work of a different Nature from any of theirs." In another place this writer adds, "They slew yr Saunchem."

This is certainly important, for it is to be observed that the opinion that the inscription upon the Dighton Rock was not the work of the Indians, was put forth more than a century before the Norse voyages to this region were discussed.

In studying the Dighton Rock, however, several difficulties present themselves. The inscription upon it has been copied at various times during the past two centuries, and the differences between the copies are many and striking. Lines appear in the later copies which one seeks for in vain in earlier ones, while in these, one finds other lines which do not exist in later copies.

This cannot be accounted for wholly upon the ground of carelessness in copying. There is too much method in some of the changes, suggesting that irreverent hands have assisted from time to time since the discovery of the rock by Europeans, in the evolution of certain figures, while nature herself has expunged and added many other lines.

This may be said to be the case with certain claimed to be Norse writings upon the Maine coast, which an old resident in the vicinity averred that he, when a boy, assisted by other boys, made upon the rocks, from time to time, for sport. Natural lines and seams were brought together and united by artificial scratches, and such additions made as comported with the fancies of the rock artists.

As for the Dighton Rock, it is in any view of the case a remarkable relic, which may well engage our attention, though we should be careful not to claim too much for it ; indeed had not the early friends of the Scandinavian theory placed so much dependence upon this and other curious relics, it is probable that they would have met with less opposition.

This opposition was active for a time, our careful historian, Bancroft, being one of the most energetic of these opponents. Perhaps it may be well to quote his own words. He says in the first chapter of his History of the United States : "The national pride of an Icelandic historian has indeed claimed for his ancestors the glory of having discovered the Western hemisphere. The geographical details are too vague to sustain a conjecture ; the accounts of the mild winter and fertile soil are on any modern hypothesis, fictions or exaggerations ; the description of the natives applies only to the Esquimaux, inhabitants of hyperborean regions ; the remark which should define the shortest winter's day has received interpretations, adapted to every latitude from New York to Cape Farewell, and Vinland has been sought in all directions from Greenland and the St. Lawrence to Africa.

Imagination has conceived the idea that vast inhabited regions lay unexplored in the West ; and poets have declared, that empires beyond the ocean would, one day, be revealed to the daring navigator.

But Columbus deserves the undivided glory of having realized that belief."[16]

Certainly, with Bancroft, we must all render homage to Columbus for his great and heroic efforts in bringing the

Western Continent to the attention of the Nations of Europe ; at the same time, we should not fail to render whatever credit may be due to those who preceded him but who made their discoveries at a time when the world was not ready to avail itself of them. This will in no wise detract from the honor due to the great Genoese navigator.

In spite, however, of all the opposition which has been made, there is to-day among historical students, an almost general consensus of opinion in favor of the validity of the Scandinavian claims, and this opinion is the result of a careful study of the documents themselves, which bear many internal evidences of their truthfulness.

Before examining them, however, let us glance briefly at a few historical facts preceding them ; the discovery of Iceland by Naddodd, and of Greenland by Erik the Red, which show what daring navigators these Northmen were.

Naddodd, a viking or piratical trader, was the first recorded discoverer of Iceland. Returning from Norway in the year 861, he was blown by a violent tempest from his course. While lost in a boundless waste of waters, he saw through the gloom the high hills of a strange land rising from the bosom of the sea, and entering a bay, afterwards known as Reider Fiord, he climbed a mountain to survey the Country, hoping to find it inhabited ; but no sign of human beings was discoverable. Three years later, one Gardar, a Swede, was driven to the same land, and wintered there.

The fame of these discoveries spread abroad, and caused an adventurous seaman named Floki to set out on its exploration. Taking with him three crows, he touched at Shetland and Faroe, and after sailing a long distance from the latter place, he let one of the birds escape, which flew away in the direction of the land left. Judging from this that Faroe[17] was still the nearest land, he continued his voyage, after a while loosing another bird, which, rising high in the air and circling about a while, returned to the ship, seeing no place whither it might fly for rest. The third bird, which he released several days later, however, flew away from the ship, and following its flight, he soon came in sight of the wished-for land.

Here he passed two winters, but becoming discouraged at the loss of his cattle, for which he had not gathered sufficient food during the summer, he returned to Norway.

The first permanent colony was planted in Iceland by Ingolf. Ingolf and Leif were cousins, whose families had long been united by common troubles, and were about to become more closely united by the marriage of Leif with Helga, the fair sister of his friend and cousin. At a feast given by the cousins to the three rough sons of Atli Jarl, with whom they had been in an evil hour co-partners in an expedition, Holmstein, one of Atli's sons, who was a rude and quarrelsome fellow, declared that he would wed Helga and none other. This led to a battle, in which Holmstein was slain.

The cousins, being shortly after attacked by another of the brothers, slew him, also, and for these acts they were banished, and set sail for the strange land which Naddodd had discovered, and of which they had often heard.

The cousins reached this land in 870. Ingolf, in the Spring of the year 871, returned to Norway to dispose of his effects there, and to get some of his friends to return with him, while Leif made a voyage to Ireland; voyages being not uncommon at this period between Norway and Ireland; whence he returned with an immense booty.

Ingolf induced many of his friends to undertake with him the foundation of a colony in this new country, and in 874, he, with a number of his countrymen, set sail from Norway without chart or compass, and boldly steered his little ship out into the broad and unknown ocean in search of a new home. Ingolf took with him the pillars of his old home, and when approaching the coast, threw them overboard, that he might be guided by them to a favorable place for his new abode. But a storm came on, and, losing them, he was obliged to land on the Southeastern shore, at a place named for him, Ingolfshofde, where he and his party erected habitations, and there remained for three years, at the end of which time, some of Ingolf's servants having found the pillars on the beach near what is known as Reikiavik, the present capital, he removed thither.

Thus was Iceland permanently settled in the year 874. It is a strange fact connected with this early settlement of Iceland, that the Landnamabok or Land Roll of the first settlers, states that they found Christians there, men called Papæ, who, it is said, came from the West over the Sea, and with them Irish books and many other things, whence it was known that they were Westmen, as the Irishmen were called.

The venerable Bede, who flourished in the eighth century, says, that in his time, expeditions were made to Iceland, and it is said that these things, meaning such things as the first settlers in Iceland found among the people they called Papæ, have been found in the Isle of Papæ, on the East coast of Iceland, and at Papylio. This shows what frequent and extensive voyages were made by Europeans at this early day.

Thus far we have followed history,[18] but from this point we will follow the Icelandic Sagas.[19]

A century after the settlement of Iceland, Erik, surnamed the Red, who, with his Father, Thorvald, had been banished from Norway for slaying a man, and who had settled in Iceland, having in his new home again killed a man in a quarrel, was banished from Iceland, and fitting out a vessel he sailed Westward in search of the Rocks of Gunniborn, rocky islands, which, it was said, one Gunniborn had seen to the West of Iceland.

Erik told his friends that if he found these islands he would re-visit them. After sailing Westward many days, he at last came in sight of land, which he spent some time in exploring. This was in the year 982. Having found a suitable spot for habitation, he set out on his return voyage, which he accomplished in safety. He gave glowing accounts of the new country which he had discovered, misnaming it Greenland, unless he named it from his credulous friends, and finally induced a number of the people, with whom he appears to have been popular, to accompany him.

He therefore set sail with twenty-five ships from Iceland ; fourteen of which only reached Greenland, the others having been lost or blown back to Iceland. Among those who accompanied Erik was Heriulf, who was a worthy descendant of Ingolf, the early settler of Iceland. This Heriulf had a son, Bjarni Heriulfson, who, when his father sailed with his friend Erik, was away in Norway.

This Bjarni, it seems, was an adventurous spirit, a thorough seaman, and possessed with a great desire to see strange lands, and at this time had obtained considerable renown and wealth. His winters were passed alternately abroad and with his father in Iceland. Coming back in the Summer to Iceland, he was surprised to find that his father and his men had gone with Erik to the new country, West, and he at once set out in search of him, saying that he meant to pass the Winter with his father as usual, wherever he was.

With Bjarni was a Christian from the Hebrides, we are told, and this man is not again alluded to, except that when passing a dangerous whirlpool, he is said to have sung a hymn. At this time Bjarni and his crew had not been converted to Christianity, and they probably regarded a Christian as somewhat of a curiosity. The very simplicity of this allusion to the man of a strange belief, and to the natural incident of his singing a hymn when in danger, may certainly be properly pointed out as one of the internal evidences of the truth of the narrative.

For three days they sailed with a fair wind, until land was lost to view, when strong Northeasterly winds sprang up, and dismal fogs prevailed. For many days they were driven forward, till at length, the weather clearing, they saw the sky again, and driving on another day they descried land. The sailors wanted to know of Bjarni if this was Greenland, but he was evidently too good a navigator to think it was, and, approaching nearer, he was well satisfied that it was not, since unlike Greenland, this country was not mountainous, which was to them a striking fact, as nearly all the countries they knew were.

This land was covered with forests and had rising ground in many parts. Leaving it to the left, they put about with the stern of the ship towards the land and sailed on this course two days, when they again saw land. The sailors asked Bjarni if this was Greenland, but he said that it could not be, " Because in Greenland are said to be very high ice hills." This land was low and thickly covered with wood. The sailors wanted to land, but the prudent Bjarni would not permit this, though they clamored loudly and tried to make him believe that they were short of wood and water.

Doubtless he was afraid that if they once landed it would take a long time to get them on board again ; besides, the season was getting late, and unknown perils were before him ; so, refusing the pressing entreaties of his men, he pushed on to the Northeast, and after three days' sailing again made land. They coasted along its shore till he perceived that it was an island. Then he put the ship about with its stern towards the land, and stood out to sea, with the wind from the Southwest, which soon increased so that they were obliged to shorten sail. So they sped on for four days, when a mountainous land appeared in sight, and this proved to be Greenland, where he found his father, and there abode with him that Winter, 985-6.   .

Of course the discovery of a land Southwest of Greenland caused a great deal of discussion, and Bjarni was much
blamed, especially in Norway, where he afterwards went, for
not pushing his exploration further. It was left, however, to
Leif, the eldest son of Erik, to attempt the voyage.

Visiting Norway in 999, Leif embraced Christianity,
under the persuasive influence of King Olaf Tryggvason.
At the Court of this monarch, the discovery of Bjarni, Leif's
friend, was doubtless often discussed and his course cen-
sured. Leif determined to attempt the voyage himself, and
with this purpose in mind, he returned to Greenland with his
men, who had all embraced Christianity. Thus in the year
999 was Christianity introduced into Greenland by Leif
Erikson, who, from what is related of him, was a man of noble
character and bearing. Reaching home, his first business was
to purchase his friend Bjarni's vessel, which, it appears, was a
good one for such a hazardous undertaking, and, with a crew
of thirty-five men, he, without chart or compass, set sail in
search of the new land which Bjarni had seen to the Southwest.

Of course he was not impelled by unselfish motives, for
rumor magnified in those days the wealth of all new countries. It is said that Erik, his father, had determined to accompany him on his dangerous voyage, but at the last
moment refused, though urgently pressed by his son, giving
as an excuse a slight accident[20] which had just happened to
him, a trifling incident, but such a one as would hardly have
been created by a romancer, who could have easily invented
something of a much more startling character. One of Leif's

crew was a man from the South country ; that is, Germany.
The name of this man was Tyrker, which signifies the German, whom we shall find further along in the narrative,
appearing in a characteristic manner.

Following the description given of his course by Bjarni,
Leif finally made land, and going ashore, examined it.
Above were frozen heights ; no herbage appeared, and the
whole space between the heights and the sea was covered
with bare flat rocks.   Leif named this forbidding country
Helluland ; that is, flat-stone-land, and then put to sea, following the track which Bjarni had described.   Rafn supposes
this to have been Newfoundland, and to one who has been
upon the coast, the description of Leif appears strikingly
accurate.   Continuing his course, Leif again made land, which
he describes as Bjarni describes it, as being flat and well wooded, though he omits the small heights which Bjarni mentions.
Leif, however, unlike Bjarni, landed and saw more.

He says that the shores were low, and that they saw
about them wide stretches of white sand, which is a very
important addition to Bjarni's statement, and tends to iden-
tify the country with Nova Scotia, as the white sands and
long, level appearance of the hills from the sea, are particularly noted by modern voyagers along the Nova Scotia coast.
The very differences in the two accounts of Bjarni and Leif
tend to establish the truthfulness of both, since these
differences naturally grow out of the different circumstances
under which they beheld the country.

"This land," said Leif, "shall be named after its qualities
and called Markland," that is, Woodland. Again they sailed

two days, when they again made land, and approaching,
touched at an island, which lay opposite the easterly part of
the main land.

They found the air remarkably pleasant, and noticed
that the grass was covered with dew, which, touching acci-
dentally and conveying to the mouth, was found to be sweet
to the taste. What was this island? Starting from the
sandy shores of Cape Sable, with a northwesterly wind, the
first land fall would probably be Cape Cod or the Island of
Nantucket. Changes are supposed to have taken place in
this region, owing to the action of the Gulf Stream, which
have reduced the prominence of the eastern portion of the
promontory, and worn away islands which formerly existed
in the vicinity.

The sweet dew mentioned may have been caused by
Aphides, and is sometimes so abundant, says Brande, as to
fall from the leaves in drops. Its existence, therefore, is not
a myth, as some critics have supposed.

Returning to the ship, they sailed into a sound which
lay between the island and the promontory, which ran out
from the land eastwardly, and steered westerly past it.
At ebb tide, the shallows were so great that, says the Saga,
"it was far to see from the ship to the water," but they were
so eager to land that they did not wait for the rising tide,
but ran on shore at a place where a river flowed out of a
lake ; but upon the flood tide they floated their ship up the
river and into the lake.

There could hardly be a more exact description made by
a person, who, after passing the promontory and the mouth

of Buzzard's Bay, should take the Seaconnet passage and
Pocasset River into Mount Hope Bay. It is said that after
counselling together, they concluded to pass the winter
there, and at once began building habitations. They
found abundance of salmon in both river and lake, and
thought that the nature of the country was such that cattle
would not require to be housed in Winter. They also observed that the day and night were more equal than in
Greenland or Iceland; the sun on the shortest day being
above the horizon from half past seven in the morning until
half past four in the afternoon.

Both of the foregoing statements have met with opposition. We have seen that Bancroft has objected, that the
description of the climate of Vinland does not apply to the
climate of Rhode Island. The exact words of the Saga are,
" They thought that the nature of the country was so good
that cattle would not require house feeding in Winter; for
there came no frost in Winter, and little did the grass wither
there. "

There can be no doubt that people coming from the icy
shores of Greenland, would find in such a locality as Mount
Hope Bay a most agreeable change from the extreme rigors
to which they had been accustomed, and would be likely
to exaggerate the mildness of the climate. A writer,
a few years since, in describing this region, has said,
that in " most winters a scanty substance might be procured
for cattle, but this could not be depended upon. Farmers
generally house their cattle in Winter. We do not consider
it absolutely necessary, though a prudent husbandman will

do it. Some individuals in that vicinity do not shelter their
sheep, and say they thrive well and become robust." [21]

With regard to the length of the day, which would indi-
cate the latitude of the place, much has been written. When
Bancroft wrote, he was probably influenced in his opinion by
the fact that Torfœus, in calculating the latitude of the place
where Leif wintered, fixed it in Newfoundland, an error
which is now known to have resulted from a misinterpre-
tation. Rafn has calculated the latitude to be 41 degrees,
24 minutes, 10 seconds, which is in the vicinity of Mount
Hope Bay. It is certainly remarkable that with their im-
perfect method of calculating time, the Norsemen should
have been so accurate in their statement.

Having "done with house building," says the narrative,
Leif divided his men into two companies, which were to take
turns daily in exploring and guarding the common property.
The exploring party was under orders to always return at
night, and never to separate. Leif, it is said, "was a great
and strong man, grave and well favored, therewith sensible
and moderate in all things."

Upon an evening when the explorers returned, it was
found that one of the party was missing. This was Tyrker,
the German. He had long been with Leif's father, and had
been loved by Leif from his childhood, hence the latter was
greatly disturbed at his absence, and sharply chided his men
for losing sight of him. Taking twelve men he started in
search of Tyrker, but had not gone far when he met the old
man returning. Leif joyfully received him, but perceived
that he was in an excited condition of mind, and enquired

why he was out so late, and how he became separated from the party. Tyrker at first repeated some German words, rolling his eyes and twisting his mouth, and then answered in Norse, "I have not been much further off, but still have I something new to tell of; I found vines and grapes." "But is that true, my foster father?" asked Leif. "Surely is it true," replied he, "for I was bred up in the land where there is no want of either wine or grapes."

This incident has been especially ridiculed, yet its simplicity is an argument in favor of its truth. Tyrker is represented as a nervous man, with a high forehead, unsteady eyes, a freckled face, and of small stature; but a skilled artisan. He had not seen grapes for many years, and the discovery of them naturally occasioned great joy. What explanation is more reasonable, than that the excitable old man should repeat in German, sayings learned in youth in praise of the grape, of which many abound in the German tongue?

The next morning Leif set his men at work gathering grapes, cutting vines and felling trees with which to load the ship. The long boat it is said he caused to be filled with grapes. "Now," says the narrative, "was a cargo cut down for the ship, and when Spring came they got ready and sailed away; and Leif gave the land a name after its qualities and called it Vinland."

Having put to sea with a fair wind, they at length came in sight of Greenland. As they approached, one of Leif's men asked him why he steered so close to the wind, and was answered, that he was doing more than steering as he saw something, but was not sure whether it was a ship or a rock. Presently however, his quick eye saw that it was a rock and men upon it.

Going to the assistance of the men, Tyrker asked, as Leif brought his ship to anchor near the rock, the name of their leader, and was told that it was Thorer, a Norwegian by birth. Thorer in turn asked the name of the Captain of the ship which had come to his rescue and was told that it was Leif the son of Erik the Red of Brattahlid. Leif then kindly took Thorer and his men, fifteen in all, on board with as many of their goods as possible and sailed for home.

Leif showed Thorer and his companions great hospitality and found employment for his men. For saving the lives of these people, as well probably as for his successful voyage, he was ever afterwards called Leif the lucky. This expedition contributed to his wealth and honor.

During the following winter, Thorer and a number of his companions fell victims to a disease which prevailed in Greenland. Erik the Red, Leif's father, died also.

Leif's successful voyage was much discussed, and Thorvald his brother thought the new country had not been sufficiently explored, whereupon Leif gave him leave to go to Vinland, loaning his ship for the voyage, upon conditions that she should first go and bring the timber which had been left upon the rock when Thorer was wrecked, which was done.

We now come to the voyage of Thorvald which took place in the Spring of 1002. Nothing is said of the incidents connected with it. We are only told that it was propitious, and that the new World was reached in due time. Thorvald found the dwellings which Leif had erected, and called them Leif's booths.   .

Having drawn their ship on shore for safety, the Norsemen passed the Winter there. In the Spring, Thorvald had the ship put in order, and sent a crew in the long boat to explore. They found the land fair and well wooded along the coast, with white sand beaches, many islands and much shallow water. The only sign of habitation they found, was a wooden shed.

The Summer was spent in exploration. The next season, Thorvald took the ship and explored the coast "eastward—and around to the land northward." This is a very significant statement, as it is the direction they would be obliged to take in explorations from this point towards the North. When off a ness, or promontory, a storm drove the ship ashore and the keel was broken from it. This Thorvald set up on the promontory and called it Kialarness or Keel point.

They then sailed round the eastern shores and into the neighboring bays, until they reached a beautifully wooded point, where Thorvald landed exclaiming " Here is beautiful and here would I like to raise my dwelling." Shortly after they discovered three skin boats or canoes, and under each of them three natives. Eight of these they killed, but one escaped and gave the alarm to his friends in the vicinity, who attacked the Norse ship in their canoes, and after a sharp battle were defeated.

Thorvald, however, received a mortal wound from an arrow. Finding he was about to die, he said to his men, "Now counsel I ye that ye get ready instantly to depart, but ye shall bear me to that Cape, where I thought it best to dwell; it may be that a true word fell from my mouth, that I should dwell there for a time ; there shall ye bury me, and set up crosses at my head and feet, and call the place Krossaness, for ever in all time to come."

" Now Thorvald died," says the Saga, "but they did all things according to his directions, and then went away, and returned to their companions, and told to each other the tidings which they knew, and dwelt there for the Winter and gathered grapes and vines to load the ship. But in the Spring, they made ready to sail to Greenland and came in their ship to Eriksfjord, and could now tell great tidings to Leif."

Thorstein, the younger son of Erik, being possessed with a desire to go to Vinland to get the body of his brother Thorvald, fitted out the ship which Thorvald had sailed in, and with twenty-five men selected for their strength and stature, and his wife Gudride set out for Vinland. Through the entire summer they were tossed about by the sea, and driven about by contrary winds. It was not till the beginning of Winter that they made land, which they found to be on the West coast of Greenland, at a place called Lysefjord.

Landing here to winter, a disease attacked his sailors, and Thorstein commanded coffins to be made for them, for said he " I will have all the bodies taken to Eriksfjord in the Summer;" but Thorstein himself fell a prey to the disease.

By the kindness of a man who dwelt at Lysefjord however, Thorstein's ship was taken back to Eriksfjord bearing Gudride and the bodies of Thorstein and those of his crew who died.

But another voyage to the new world was to be made. In the Autumn of the year in which Gudride returned to Brattahlid, that is, in 1006, there came Thorfinn Karlsefne in his ship from Iceland. Becoming enamored of the fair widow he wooed and married her during the Winter.

The discourse at Brattahlid often turned upon the discovery of Vinland the Good, and many thought that a profitable voyage might be made thither ; hence, in the Spring, three vessels were made ready for the expedition. Thorfinn took command of his own ship, and was accompanied by Gudride and other friends. Snorri Thorbrandson, a man of distinguished lineage, commanded one of the vessels ; another was commanded by Bjarni Grimolfson, and Thorhall Gamlason who had passed the Christmas at Brattahlid, and the ship in which Thorbjorn, Gudride's father, formerly came from Iceland was made ready, and put under command of Thorward, a son-in-law of Erik, who took with him his wife Freydis. The minuteness of the account is striking. The ship which brought Thorbjorn from Iceland, was an old one, as the event occurred many years before, and bears so little upon the narrative as to render it improbable that a romancer would introduce it into his story. It seems, indeed, like one of the little details of a simple and truthful history.

They first sailed to Westerbygd, and thence in a southerly direction to Helluland, where they found foxes abund-

ant ; and then still southerly for two days, when they reached Markland, which was well wooded, as before mentioned by
their predecessors.   In this account is added to the description of Markland, that it was well stocked with animals.
Thus by putting the various accounts together of the places
mentioned in the Sagas, we find that they more completely
describe the places we have supposed them to refer to, a fact
which greatly strengthens our belief in their historical accuracy.

Leaving Markland they sailed South for two days and
then turned to the southeast, and "found a land covered
with wood, and many wild beasts upon it : an island lay there
out from the land to the southeast ; there killed they a bear
and called the place Bear Island, but the land Markland."
This island is an important addition to the account, and well
applies to Cape Sable Island.

"Thence sailed they far to the Southward along the
land and came to a ness ; the land lay upon the right ; they
landed and found there upon the ness the keel of a ship"
and recognized it as Kialarness.   The strands they called
Fdurdudstrands, the Wonderstrands, on account of their extent and appearance.

This is another important addition to the former des-
criptions and well identifies Cape Cod.   Let us read Hitch-
cock's description of the Cape.   "The dunes, or sand hills,
which are often nearly or quite barren of vegetation and of
snowy whiteness, forcibly attract attention on account of
their peculiarity.   As we approached the extremity of the
Cape, the sand and barrenness increased ; and in not a few

places, it would need only a party of Bedouin Arabs to cross the traveller's path, to make him feel that he was in the depths of an Arabian or Lybian desert."[22]

It has been claimed by Dr. Kohl, the eminent historian, that Thorfinn in sailing from Nova Scotia to Cape Cod, sailed along the coast of Maine. He translates the account of this part of the voyage thus: "They coasted along a great-way *to the Southwest having the land always on their starboard until they came to Kialarness.*"[23] This is an erroneous rendering of the passage, which is as we have quoted it, namely "Thence sailed they far to the southward along the land, and came to a ness; the land lay upon the right."

It is certainly quite evident that there is not the least ground in the Sagas upon which to found Dr. Kohl's theory, which seems to be the result of a careless rendering of the original, by which it is made to appear that they sailed southward along the shore with the land always upon their right until they reached the Cape. To any one who will study the conformation of the coast, it will be seen that this theory is wholly untenable.

The narrative continues that the land became indented with coves, one of which they entered with the ship. King Olaf Tryggvason had given Thorfinn two Scots, a man and a woman, who were swift of foot. These he put ashore very lightly clad, with orders to run over the country to the southward for three days, and to then return. When they returned to the ship, they brought with them a bunch of grapes and an ear of corn to show what the land produced.

Proceeding on their course, the ships reached a frith where lay an island, around which were powerful currents.

The eider ducks were so plenty upon this island, that one could hardly walk upon it without breaking the eggs of those birds. They called the island Straumey, or the Isle of currents. This whole account points to the Isle of Martha's Vineyard, or Cuttyhunk as the Straumey of the Norsemen. The currents here are still strong and rapid and are due to the Gulf Stream. The Islands in this vicinity were formerly so much frequented by wild fowl as to have been called Egg Islands. The very fact that Leif and Thorvald did not mention these rapid currents is significant, that they passed across the mouth of, while Thorfinn sailed up Buzzard's Bay.

This bay, Thorfinn called Straumfjord or Bay of currents. Here they disembarked and made preparations for passing the Winter. They had brought cattle for which they found pasturage and passed the Winter of 1007-8. They spent considerable time in explorations, and fishing declining, they were short of food for which they prayed to God, but their prayers were not answered.

Thorhall having absented himself from them, they sought and found him on a rock looking up to the sky and murmuring something. This was shortly explained when they found near by the body of a whale, which, Thorhall, who was not a Christian, claimed was sent in answer to his verses to Thor and not by Christ in answer to the Christians' prayer. The flesh of the whale had made them sick, and when they heard Thorhall's claim they cast the flesh of the whale back into the sea. The weather now improved; they were able to get fish and eggs from the island as well as game. Thorhall

now wanted to cruise northward, while Thorfinn preferred
to explore southward, hence they separated, but only eight
men accompanied Thorhall.   It is said they were overtaken
by a storm and blown to the Irish Coast, where they were
made slaves.

Thorfinn, however, and the others sailed southward
along the coast and came to a river which "ran out from the
land through a lake into the sea."   It was very shallow and
one could not enter the river without high water.   They
sailed up as far as the mouth and called the place Hop.   On
the low lands they found wild wheat, growing, while on the
high lands were vines.

The name given by the Norsemen to this Bay is noticeable.   It signifies a recess formed by the confluence of a
river and the sea, and perfectly describes Mount Hope Bay.
We know that Indian words were frequently anglicised ; as
in the instance of Pjepscot, which was transformed into
Bishop's Cot.   Latin scholars gave them a Latin form, as in
the case of Lacadia, which became Acadia, and Frenchmen
transformed them into French words, which they resembled
in sound.   This was the case with the Indian word, Haup,
which was metamorphosed into Hopé.   The question naturally arises, was the Indian name Haup derived from the
Norse residents there, and so handed down?   Whether this
is true or not, the coincidence is remarkable.   The
Norsemen applied to the bay, which they described, and
which answers perfectly to the description of Mount Hope
Bay as before said, the name Hop ; the Indians called it
Haup, and it is on maps to-day, *Hope*, certainly a noticeable
coincidence.

Another coincidence is quite noticeable. The Norsemen called the Cape, which they described a ness, or naze, and Cape Cod was called by the Indians Nesset or Nauset. Thorfinn's men found fish abundant in Hop Bay. By digging holes near the shores they took many flat fish which were left by the receding tide.

They passed half a month in this pleasant place, having moved hither their cattle and other property. One morning they were surprised to see a number of canoes filled with savages coming around the Cape from the South. Thorfinn raised up a white shield in token of peace. The natives who are described as being swarthy and ill favored, with coarse hair, large eyes and broad cheeks, gazed at them for a while in surprise, and then rowed away in the direction in which they came.

Thorfinn and his people erected dwellings about the Lake and passed the Winter there; but on the appearance of Spring they were again surprised one morning to see a large number of canoes coming around the Cape from the South. Thorfinn, as before, raised a white shield, and the Natives soon opened a barter, exchanging furs for red cloth, which they greatly coveted. They also wanted swords and spears, which Thorfinn refused to let them have. For a bit of red cloth they gave a whole skin, and when the supply of the precious cloth ran low, it was cut up into still smaller bits and dealt out to them. Those who obtained strips of it bound it about their heads.

Thorfinn finally treated them to some milk soup, which they relished so well, that they gave back the red cloth for it,

and the chronicler says quaintly, "the traffic of the Skræl-
ings wound up by their bearing away their purchases in
their stomachs ; but Karlsefne and his companions retained
their goods and skins." It happened that a bull belonging
to the Norsemen ran from the woods bellowing, which greatly terrified the Savages, who fled in dismay. They were not
again seen for three weeks, and then they reappeared in
great numbers. A battle took place, which resulted in the
retreat of the Savages. Thorfinn had lost some of his men
in the fight, and although the country was good, they ap-
prehended danger from the natives ; therefore they thought
best to depart.

They sailed northward along the Coast, and surprised
five natives clothed in skins. They had with them vessels
containing marrow mixed with blood. Thorfinn supposed
them to be exiles from their people, and his men killed them.
They afterwards came to a promontory abounding in wild
animals as they judged from marks which they saw. If we
have followed the Norsemen thus far correctly, this promontory should be the one upon which the city of Providence
now stands. From here they went to Straumfjord, where
they found abundance of food. Thorfinn now went West in
his ship in search of Thorhall, leaving the other ship and
crew at Straumfjord. Sailing northward around Kialarness,
they went westward after passing that promontory, the land
laying to the left.

When they had sailed for some time they came to a
river which "fell out of the land from east to west ; they put
in to the mouth of the river, and lay by its southern bank."

Not finding Thorhall they returned to Kialarness, from whence they sailed southward. The hills, which they saw as they sailed, they considered as being a part of the same range which they had seen at Hop.

This statement should be particularly noted, as it forms an important link in the chain of evidence which we have adduced in support of the accuracy with which the Sagas describe Cape Cod and the regions laying both to the North and Southwest of that remarkable headland.

The winter of 1009–10 was passed at Straumfjord. During the first Autumn of their arrival a son had been born to Thorfinn, whom he named after his friend Snorri, and he was now in his third year. In the Spring of 1010, they set sail for Vinland, touching at Markland, where they surprised several natives and succeeded in capturing two boys, whom they took to Eriksfjord where they were taught the Norse language and baptized.

The other ship which accompanied Thorfinn, and which was commanded by Bjarni Grimolfson, was blown eastward and lost; a few only of the crew escaped in an open boat. In the Spring, Thorfinn and Gudride sailed for Norway, where they were received with great honor. The furs which Thorfinn had obtained from the natives were considered of much value.

The next season they departed from Norway for Iceland and passed the Winter at Reynisness. The next Spring, Thorfinn bought the Glaumbæ estate, and there passed the rest of his life.

We now come again to authentic history, having span-
ned a gap with the Sagas.   The family of Thorfinn was
illustrious in Iceland and his descendants numerous, many of
them becoming well known in Scandinavian history.   Gudride and Snorri—the son born in the new world—lived on
his estate after the death of Thorfinn ; but when Snorri
married, his mother took a voyage to Rome.   During her
absence Snorri, who was a devout Christian, built a church
at Glaumbæ.   After her return from Rome, Gudride remained with her son at Glaumbæ for awhile, and then entered a
convent, where she passed the remainder of her life.

The next voyage to Vinland was made in 1011, and
from this time voyages thither became frequent.   In 1059 it
is said that an Irish priest named John went there to Christ-
ianize the natives and was murdered by them, while Erik,
called the first bishop of Greenland, is also said to have sailed for Vinland in 1121.

The latest account is of a voyage to Markland in 1347
by a ship from Greenland.   By this it is seen that intercourse with Vinland was kept up until the middle of the
fourteenth century.

This brings us near the date of the voyage claimed to
have been made to the Western Continent by Nicolo Zeno,
in 1380.   The Venetians made frequent voyages to the
North of Europe at this time, and had commercial intercourse with the Scandinavians.

On the famous map, made after his return by Zeno, and
which he hung up in his palace at Venice, a map which has
been the subject of much curious study to geographers for

centuries, is depicted not only Greenland and the Faroe Isles, but the coast of America. This map, it should be remembered, was in existence in Venice long before the voyage of Columbus was undertaken.

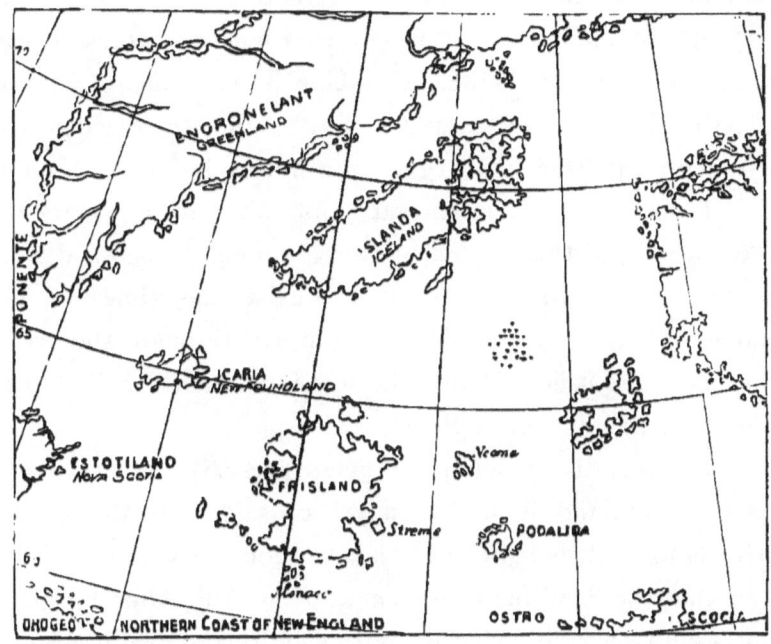

It will of course be asked why the Norse did not permanently colonize the new world. Large colonies could not have been established by them at this period, and if small ones were established it is probable that the colonists perished or amalgamated with the natives, for about the year 1350, they must have been cut off entirely from the Greenland Colonies.

About this time, the pestilence known as the black death raged through Europe with fatal violence, almost depopulating vast districts, and is supposed to have raged in Greenland and greatly diminished its scattered population. It is known to have been most fatal at Trondheim, where it was introduced by an English ship, and this port held the principal trade of Greenland.   Intercourse was entirely cut off with Greenland, and it is said that natives attacked the colony in 1379 and killed eighteen of the inhabitants of Westbygd and carried away two boys, and that when assistance went from Eastbygd, not a human being was found.

Torfæus says, that no attempt was made to regain Westbygd, and that the natives or Esquimaux occupied it in peace.   The Eastbygd continued to exist sometime longer, and some intercourse with it continued through the 15th century when it ceased, and the few inhabitants either perished or amalgamated with the natives.

The records which have been preserved of the voyages to Vinland, it has already been said, were discovered in Iceland. and their preservation is doubtless due to the fact, that this land being so remote from the church, after Christianity was introduced there, such records were permitted to exist by the native priests, who were of, and sympathized with the people ; while in countries nearer the central power of the Church every ancient record was ruthlessly destroyed.

Anderson says, "for ages Iceland was destined to become the sanctuary and preserver of the grand old literature of the North.   Paganism prevailed there more than a century after the island became inhabited ; the old traditions were cherished and committed to memory, and shortly after

the introduction of Christianity the Norse Literature
was put in writing. The ancient literature and traditions of
Iceland, excel anything of the kind in Europe during the
middle ages. The original Teutonic life lived longer and
more independently in Norway, and especially in Iceland,
than elsewhere, and had more favorable opportunities to
grow and mature, and the Icelandic literature is the full
blown flower of Teutonic heathendom. This Teutonic
heathendom, with its beautiful and poetical mythology, was
rooted out by superstitious priests in Germany and the other
countries inhabited by Teutonic peoples, before it had de-
veloped sufficiently to produce blossoms, excepting in England, where a kindred branch of the Gothic race rose to
eminence in letters, and produced the Anglo Saxon literature."[24]

It is to be noted, that in the account of the voyage
of Thorfinn it is said, that Gudride after the death of her
husband, made a pilgrimage to Rome. Gudride was greatly
interested in the new world, having attempted a voyage
thither with her first husband, and afterwards having accompanied her second husband, Thorfinn, thither, and she
doubtless related her experiences at the Court of Rome.

The Pope was greatly interested in learning of new
lands, which he could add to his jurisdiction, and he took
great pains to collect reports and charts of such lands.
Pontifical documents, the contents of which have come down
to our times, reveal to us the course which Christianity pur-
sued westward. Thus in 830, Pope Gregory IV. confirmed
Auscarius as the first Archbishop of Hamburg. In 860,

Pope Nicholas invested him as his legate, with jurisdiction "over the Swedes, Danes and Slafs, as well as over any other nations in those parts." Eighty-eight years later, Pope Agapetus granted similar jurisdiction to Archbishop Adalgarus over Swedes, Danes and *Norwegians*. In 1022, Pope Benedict VIII. granted the same over Swedes, Danes, Norwegians and *Icelanders*. This is the first mention of Iceland in the pontifical documents. Thirty-one years later, Pope Leo IX. confirmed these powers to Archbishop Adelbert over Swedes, Danes, Norwegians, Icelanders, Laplanders and over *Greenland*.[25] This is the first mention of Greenland in the pontifical documents, while we learn that in 1121 Erik Upsi was granted similar powers over the countries before mentioned, and in addition, *Vinland*. It is said that in 1121 Erik Upsi was appointed Bishop of Iceland, Greenland and Vinland.

It is also acknowledged that Columbus was in Iceland in the year 1477, fifteen years before the discovery of America. The most remarkable record perhaps, and one which it seems Columbus must have seen, since he was a student and eager to obtain knowledge of new countries, is that of Adam of Bremen, who died in the year 1076. His book on the "Propagation of the Christian Religion in the North of Europe" was published in 1073 and read by educated men throughout Europe.

At the end of this book is a geographical treatise entitled, "On the position of Denmark and other regions beyond Denmark," and having given an account of Denmark, Sweden, Norway, Iceland and Greenland, the author says, "Besides

these, there is still another region, which has been visited by
many, lying in that ocean, which is called Vinland, because
vines grow there spontaneously, producing very good wine;
corn likewise springs up there without being sown," and
"*This we know not by fabulous conjecture, but from positive
statements of the Danes.*"[26]

NOTES.

1. Vide Athanasii Kircheri E. Soc. Jesu. Œdipus Ægyptiacus.
Romæ, MDCLII, p. 421, et seq.
2. Vide Enquiries touching the Diversity of Languages and
Religions through the Chief Parts of the World. By Edward Brerewood, London, MDCLXXIV, p. 117.
3. Vide Histoire de la Nouvelle France, Par Marc Lescarbot.
Paris, 1866, Vol.1, p. 23 et seq.
4. Vide Memoires de Litterature Tires des Registres, De L'Aca-
demie Royale des Inscriptions, a Paris, MDCCLXI, Vol. 28, pp. 503–
525.
5. It is perhaps worth while to state that in the audience which
listened to the reading of this paper by the author, at Columbia College
in 1888, was Prince Roland Bonaparte, who was attending a session of the
Authropological Society. At the close of the reading, the Prince greatly
interested those present by drawing with considerable facility upon the
blackboard, representations of symbolical figures with which he had
been familiar in China and which he stated he had been surprised to
find depicted upon ancient monuments in Mexico. From this he inferred
a connection at some period in the past between the people of China
and the southwestern shores of the North American Continent.
6. See these depicted in Pre-historic Races of the United States of
America. By J. W. Foster, LL. D., Chicago, 1874.
7. Vide Ibid, p. 97.
8. Vide Monumenta Germaniæ Historica. Edited by Henry Pertz
Hannoveræ, 1846. Though written as stated previous to 1073, the work of
Adam Von Bremen was not printed until 1579.
9. Vide The Heimskringla, or Chronicle of the Kings of Norway,
by Snorro Sturleson. Translated by Samuel Laing, Esq., London, 1844.
This allusion to the subject is as follows:—"The same writer was Leif,
the son of Eric the Red, with King Olaf, in good repute, and embraced
Christianity. But the summer that Gissur went to Iceland, King Olaf

sent Leif to Greenland, in order to make known Christianity there. He sailed the same summer to Greenland. He found, in the sea, some people on a wreck and helped them; the same time discovered he Vinland the good, and came in harvest to Greenland. He had with him a priest and other clerks, and went to dwell at Brattahlid with Erik, his father. Men called him Leif the Lucky; but Erik, his father, said that these two things went one against the other, inasmuch as Leif had saved the crew of the ship, but brought evil men to Greenland, namely the priests."

10. Vide Historia Vinlandiae Antiquae, etc., Per Thormodum Torfæum, Hafniæ, 1705.

11. Vide Antiquitates Americanæ Edidit Societas Regia Antiquariorium Septentrionalum. Studio et opera Caroli Christiani Rafn, Hafniae, 1845.

12. The following is an extract from a letter to the author from Amos Perry, Esq., of Providence, Superintendent of the Census of Rhode Island in 1885. "When this date was inserted, I had before me the first two propositions clearly established, and the following statement from Peter Easton's Diary of August 28, 1675:—"On Saturday night, forty years after the great storm in 1635, came much the like storm, blew down our wind mill and did much harm." I knew that the mill destroyed was built of wood and belonged to the colonists, and hence was called *our* wind mill, while Arnold called his building *my* stone built wind mill. The former erected in 1663 by the colonists was blown down about the last of August, 1675. Of the latter, I believe our first information is derived from a Record of the Arnold family, dated July 13, 1677, which may be found in the New England Genealogical Register, 1, 1879, page 429. An inference (not however conclusive) may be drawn from Easton's language and the condition of the place, that our (i. e. the colonists) wind mill was the only one at Newport at that date. In the absence of information on this point, we are led to infer that the destruction of the town mill gave rise to the Arnold mill, which in that case, could not have been completed before 1676, though the inferences from admitted facts, and from the absence of positive information, point to 1676 as the date of the erection of the Stone Mill."

AMOS PERRY,
Superintendent of the Census of 1885.

13. Vide Mourt's Relation edited by Henry Martyn Dexter, Boston, 1865, pp. 32-34.

14. We are indebted for the cut of the Dighton Rock here shown to the kindness of Capt. J. W. D. Hall, Secretary of the Old Colony Historical Society, Taunton, Mass. It is doubtless the best deliniation of this celebrated relic which has yet been produced. The reader should compare it with those made by Danforth in 1680; Cotton Mather in 1712; Greenwood in 1730; Sewall in 1768; Winthrop in 1778; Baylies and Goodwin in 1790; Kendall in 1807; Gardner in 1812 and the Rhode Island His-

torical Society in 1830, all depicted in the Antiquitates Americanæ of Rafn before mentioned. Dighton Rock is now in possession of the above society.

15. Vide The North American Review for 1838, pp. 161–203.

16. Vide History of the United States. By George Bancroft, Boston, 1841, Vol. I., p. 56.

17. Dicuil in De Mensura Orbis Terræ, shows that the Faroe Islands were known to the Irish as early as 725 and Iceland in 795. Vide Antiquitanes Americanæ, p. 204.

18. Vide History of the Voyages and Discoveries made in the North, by John Reinhold Forster, Dublin, 1786. Also History of the Northmen and Danes and Norsemen from the Earliest Times, etc. By Henry Wheaton, London, 1831.

19. For an excellent translation of the Sagas reference may be made to Voyages of the Northmen to America, Prince Society, Boston, 1877. Edited by the Reverend Edmund F. Slafter, A. M.

20. In going to the ship the horse which he had mounted, stumbled causing the old man to fall off and bruise his foot, which discouraged him from attempting the voyage.

21. Dr. Thomas H. Webb, secretary of the Rhode Island Historical Society, in Antiquitates Americanæ, p. 368.

22. Vide Report on the Geology of Massachusetts, p. 96, et seq.

23. Vide Documentary History of the State of Maine by J. G. Kohl, Portland, 1869, Vol. 1. p. 71.

24. Vide An Historical Sketch of the Discovery of America by the Norsemen, by Rasmus B. Anderson, A. M., Chicago, 1874, p. 56, et seq.

25. Vide Migne's Patrology of the Latin Fathers, Vols. 119, 133, 139, 143. Archbishop Adelbert was raised to the see of Hamburg in 1045 and died in 1072. Adam of Bremen says of him, that, "he was so gentle, so generous, so hospitable, so desirous of divine and human glory, that little Bremen, having become known by his virtue like another Rome, was devoutly resorted to from all quarters of the earth, especially from the North. Among the comers were Icelanders, Greenlanders and Arcadians, who came to ask for preachers." Vide Gesta Pontificum Ecclesiæ Hamburgensis. Book III., ch. 33; also cf. Book IV., ch. 36.

26. Vide Monumenta Germaniæ Historica, edited by George Henry Pertz, Haunoverœ, 1846. Tome VII. The following is perhaps nearer the original. Adam speaking of his friend and patron Adelbert says, "He spoke also of another island found in that ocean called *Winland*, because vines grow there spontaneously, yielding excellent wine. For that fruit grew there spontaneously we know not by fabulous report, but for certain, from the reports of the Danes."

www.ingramcontent.com/pod-product-compliance
Lightning Source LLC
Chambersburg PA
CBHW030904260626

47169CB00008B/2680